The Urbana Free Library

To renew: call **217-367-4057**
or go to **urbanafreelibrary.org**
and select **My Account**

BY SAVINA COLLINS

ILLUSTRATED BY
ANITA DUFALLA

SAD

Rourke
Educational Media
rourkeeducationalmedia.com

Scan for Related Titles
and Teacher Resources

Before & After Reading Activities

Teaching Focus:

Concepts of Print: Ending Punctuation- Have students locate the ending punctuation for sentences in the book. Count how many times a period, question mark, or exclamation point is used. Which one is used the most? What is the purpose for each ending punctuation mark? Practice reading these sentences with appropriate expression.

Before Reading:

Building Academic Vocabulary and Background Knowledge

Before reading a book, it is important to set the stage for your child or student by using pre-reading strategies. This will help them develop their vocabulary, increase their reading comprehension, and make connections across the curriculum.

1. Read the title and look at the cover. *Let's make predictions about what this book will be about.*
2. Take a picture walk by talking about the pictures/photographs in the book. Implant the vocabulary as you take the picture walk. Be sure to talk about the text features such as headings, the Table of Contents, glossary, bolded words, captions, charts/diagrams, or index.
3. Have students read the first page of text with you then have students read the remaining text.
4. Strategy Talk – use to assist students while reading.
   - Get your mouth ready
   - Look at the picture
   - Think…does it make sense
   - Think…does it look right
   - Think…does it sound right
   - Chunk it – by looking for a part you know
5. Read it again.

Content Area Vocabulary
Use glossary words in a sentence.

move
neighbors
sad
together

After Reading:

Comprehension and Extension Activity

After reading the book, work on the following questions with your child or students in order to check their level of reading comprehension and content mastery.

1. *What happens when Kim moves away? (Summarize)*
2. *What does Carlos's dad tell him? (Asking Questions)*
3. *How do you feel when you are sad? (Text to self connection)*
4. *How can you make others not feel sad? (Asking Questions)*

Extension Activity

Find a large sheet of paper and draw three circles in a row. In the center circle draw or paste a picture of something that makes you sad. In the next circle draw or paste pictures of people and things that make you feel better while you are feeling sad. In the third circle draw or paste things that can help you feel happier.

TABLE OF CONTENTS

BEST FRIENDS

This is Carlos.

His best friend's name is Kim.

Carlos and Kim are **neighbors.**

They play **together.**

SAD

One day, Kim tells Carlos she has to **move**.

Carlos is **sad.**

9

He says goodbye to Kim.

OVERS

Tears tickle his eyes. His belly feels sick.

Dad says it is okay to be sad.

"You will make new friends," he tells Carlos.

NEW FRIENDS

Ding dong! The doorbell rings.

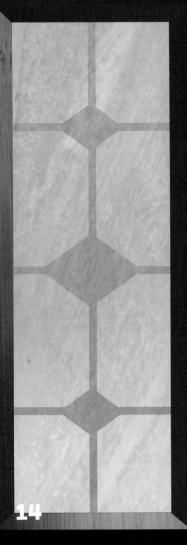
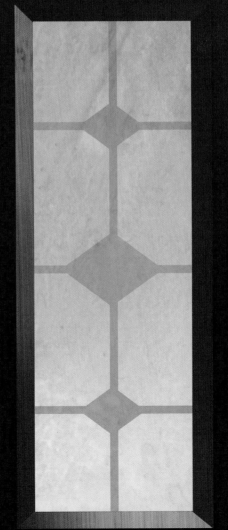

Carlos opens the door.

"I am your new neighbor Ben!"

Ben tells Carlos he did not want to move.

"I was sad to leave my friends," Ben says.

Carlos puts his arm around Ben.

"You will make new friends," Carlos says.

"I already have!" Ben smiles.

PICTURE GLOSSARY

 **move** (moov): To change the place you live.

 **neighbors** (nay-burs): People who live next door to each other.

 **sad** (sad): When you are sad, you feel unhappy.

 **together** (tuh-geTH-ur): Doing an activity with one another.

ABOUT THE AUTHOR

Savina Collins lives in Florida with her husband and 5 adventurous kids. She loves watching her kids surf at the beach. When she is not at the beach, Savina enjoys reading and taking long walks.

Meet The Author!
www.meetREMauthors.com

Library of Congress PCN Data

Sad/ Savina Collins
(I Have Feelings!)
ISBN 978-1-68342-142-9 (hard cover)
ISBN 978-1-68342-184-9 (soft cover)
ISBN 978-1-68342-215-0 (e-Book)
Library of Congress Control Number: 2016956582

Rourke Educational Media
Printed in the United States of America, North Mankato, Minnesota

www.rourkeeducationalmedia.com

Edited by: Keli Sipperley
Cover design and interior design by: Rhea Magaro-Wallace

Also Available as:

ROURKE'S e-Books